WITHDRAWN

E-2 Rarick

Jeanie's Valentine

DATE DUE

JY 25 '8	MR 02 '9	MR 3 '0
AG 17 '83		FE 13 '0
AG 17 '85	Y 17 '97	FE 11
AP 18	AG 13 '98	
FE 4 '8	FE 15 01	
MR 13 '9	FE 18 '02	
AG 21 '93	FE 26 0	
JA 12 '94		
JY 14 '9	FE 2	
AG 14 '95	FE 07 0	
FE 23 '96		

JEANIE'S VALENTINES

Follett Publishing Company

Chicago, Illinois

Atlanta, Georgia • Dallas, Texas
Sacramento, California • Warrensburg, Missouri

JEANIE'S VALENTINES

Carrie Rarick

Illustrated by Diana Magnuson

Library of Congress Cataloging in Publication Data

Rarick, Carrie.
  Jeanie's valentines.

  Summary: Because she moves to a new town just before Valentine's Day, Jeanie wonders how she will celebrate without her old school friends.
  [1. Valentine's Day—Fiction. 2. Moving, Household—Fiction] I. Title.
PZ7.R18146Je   [E]   82–2351
ISBN 0–695–41674–X   AACR2
ISBN 0–695–31674–5 (pbk.)

First Printing

Jeanie and her friends walked down the street from school.

"Just think," said Tom. "Valentine's Day is almost here. I can hardly wait."

Jeanie didn't say anything. She just looked at the sidewalk.

"I already bought my valentines," said Karla.

"I'm not buying any. I'm making all of mine this year," said Tom.

"What about you, Jeanie?" asked Karla. "Are you buying your valentines or making them?"

Jeanie's eyes filled with tears.

7

8

"What's the matter, Jeanie?" asked Tom.

"I'm thinking about what my mom and dad told me last night," said Jeanie. "They said that we're moving to Webb City soon. My dad just got a new job there. I won't be here for Valentine's Day."

Tom and Karla looked at Jeanie.

"But Jeanie," said Karla, "Webb City is far away."

"I know," said Jeanie. "I know."

Jeanie walked slowly up the stairs to her house. She always ran up those steps. But not today. Today Jeanie didn't feel like running.

Jeanie's sitter, Mrs. Downs, was waiting for Jeanie in the kitchen. Mrs. Downs had put out milk and an apple for Jeanie's after-school snack. Jeanie always gobbled down her snack. But not today. Jeanie didn't feel like eating today.

She put her head down on the kitchen table.

"It's for sure, Mrs. Downs," said Jeanie. "We really are going to move to Webb City. My dad did get that job. And I won't even be here long enough to give my friends their valentines. It will be the worst Valentine's Day I've ever had."

"Well, why don't you make your school friends their valentines right now?" said Mrs. Downs. "You can have your teacher pass them out for you on Valentine's Day. Come on. I'll help you get the things you'll need."

Mrs. Downs helped Jeanie find the things to make the valentines. They got glue, scissors, crayons, a pencil, and red paper.

They put everything on the desk in Jeanie's room. Then Jeanie began cutting out red hearts.

When Jeanie went to bed that night, her mom and dad tucked her in. They turned out the light and said good night. Jeanie always smiled when her mom and dad said good night to her. But not tonight. Jeanie didn't feel like smiling tonight.

Jeanie was thinking about moving. She didn't want to move. She didn't want to leave her house. She didn't want to leave her room. She didn't want to leave the tree outside her window. Robins had built a nest in that tree last summer.

17

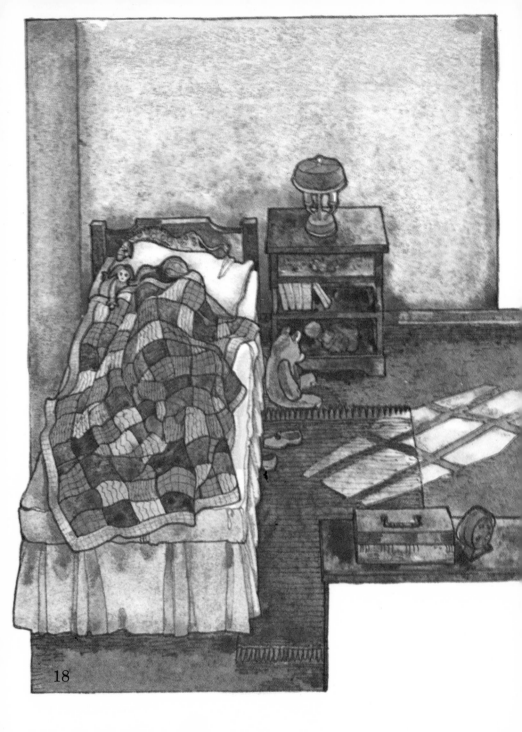

She didn't want to leave her teacher. She didn't want to leave her friends. Jeanie began to cry.

She cried until her pillow felt wet. She cried until her face felt hot and sticky. She cried until she fell asleep.

The next day was Saturday. Jeanie worked on her valentines all afternoon. She wanted them to be the best valentines she ever made. When she finished, she put her cards into a bag.

On Monday Jeanie gave the bag to her teacher, Mr. Soto. He said that he would pass out Jeanie's valentines on Valentine's Day.

Two days later was moving day.
Jeanie saw the big moving van drive up
to the house. She felt sad as she
watched the van being loaded. Then she
and her mom and dad got into their car.
They drove to their new home in Webb
City.

When Jeanie saw her new house, she began to smile. It reminded her of the house she had just left. And her room was nice and cheery. It had yellow walls and tall windows. There was a big tree outside one window. Jeanie hoped that robins would build a nest in that tree next summer.

The next week Jeanie's mom took her to her new school.

The teacher, Mrs. Price, welcomed Jeanie. And a girl named Jody showed her where to hang her coat. Then a boy named Luis showed Jeanie where to sit.

The day went by quickly. Before Jeanie knew it, the bell was ringing to go home. Mrs. Price gave Jeanie a name list.

"This will help you learn the names of the children in the class," Mrs. Price said.

Jeanie could hardly wait to get home. She ran down the sidewalk. Jeanie had not felt like running for a long time. But today she almost flew.

"I have a name list for my new class," Jeanie told her mom. "And tomorrow is Valentine's Day. I'm going to make valentines for everyone in my new class."

The next day Jeanie felt happy. She gave a valentine to everyone in the class. And everyone gave her one, too.

When she got home, there was a fat envelope in the mailbox. The envelope was full of valentines. The boys and girls in Jeanie's class at her old school had sent her cards.

That night at bedtime, Jeanie's mom and dad tucked her in bed.

Jeanie said to them, "Moving wasn't so bad after all. I have friends at my old school. I have friends at my new school. And all my friends gave me valentines. This is the best Valentine's Day I've ever had."

"We're happy that you're happy," Jeanie's mom and dad told her. Then they turned out the light and said good night. Jeanie smiled.

She smiled until her pillow stopped feeling cold. She smiled until her face felt warm and happy. She smiled until she fell asleep.

Carrie Rarick is a free-lance writer and a former teacher of young children.

In addition to giving practice with words that most children will recognize, *Jeanie's Valentines* uses the 38 enrichment words listed below.

afternoon	drove	mailbox	tucked
almost		matter	
already	enough	moving	valentines
anything	envelope		
asleep	everything	outside	waiting
			warm
bedtime	finished	pencil	welcomed
bought		pillow	worst
built	glue		
buying	gobbled	reminded	
		robins	
cheery	hearts		
crayons		scissors	
	kitchen	sidewalk	
		snack	
		sticky	